DEDICATION

To all children big and small and to all adults who are too sensible to ever grow up and still believe in Santa Claus.

CONTENTS

ACKNOWLEDGMENTS

Without the smiles and joy of all the children I see each Christmas when I adopt the roll of Santa Claus, this book would not have been written.

1   'BINDLEWITH' THE PROBLEM ELF

It's not easy being an elf.   At least that's what Santa's elf friends tell him. It is especially hard being 'Bindlewith'.   He is one of those elves who always want to do something else or be somewhere else.   If he is busy making some new Lego he would rather be helping in the Furby workshop.

If he was feeding the Reindeer, he would rather be in Santa's office checking the Christmas letters sent to him by children all over the world.

Don't get me wrong, he is a wonderful elf with a heart of gold and would do anything for anyone.   It is just that he is so restless and always wants to try something new.   Like the day when he didn't see why it was the elf and fairy bakers who had all the fun making the party cakes and decided to try to make a big cake all by himself.

He had just started and had added flour, sugar and eggs to the mixing bowl and was about to switch on the whirly mixy machine that the bakers used to make dough, when Santa came into the kitchen.   He leant over to see what 'Bindlewith' was up to, just when he switched on the machine. Well!   It took half an hour to untangle Santa's beard from the beaters.

Another day he tried to make honeycomb, or cinder toffee as some people call it, and got the mix of sugar and honey a bit wrong.   It took the elves who tried it about ten hours to unstick their teeth.
Then there was the time that 'Bindlewith' decided to spice up the Reindeer food and added too much bran to the mix.   The Reindeer thought that it was wonderful but it gave them severe windypops and we all had to wear a clothes peg on our noses for two days until the effects wore off.

As I said, 'Bindlewith' would do anything for anyone but sometimes he just tries too hard to do too much for too many and comes very unstuck.

His worst scrape so far was when the Good Fairy paid a visit and 'Bindlewith' decided to make custard for the party which was to be held later in her honour.   I won't go into detail but it was so lumpy and burnt that he tried to get rid of it down the kitchen sink.   The custard blocked the drain and he picked up the first thing that came to hand to clear it, the Good Fairy's magic wand which she had laid down when she came into the kitchen to say hello to the elves who were preparing the food for the party.

Now, I don't know how much you know about magic wands.   But they don't like being messed about with and they have a mind of their own.

'Bindlewith' poked the end of the wand down the plug hole into the mess of lumpy burnt custard. This did not please the wand one little bit and with a flash and a bang, the wand promptly turned the unfortunate elf into a slimy toad.

Poor 'Bindlewith' was left hopping about for two days just eating flies and worms until the Good Fairy took pity on him and turned him back into an elf.

Christmas Eve was approaching and all was being made ready for Santa's trip round the world to deliver the presents. The sleigh was ready. The last of the presents had been loaded and 'Bindlewith' was fussing around trying to help but he was only falling over his own feet in his eagerness and getting in everybody's way. Santa decided that if Christmas was going to happen then something would have to be found for 'Bindlewith' to do, to keep him out of the way until everything had been completed.

Santa had been having trouble with one family, the Turnbulls. Mr and Mrs Turnbull had four children. Two girls, Emma and Caroline and two boys, Simon and Mark. Oh! And I nearly forgot the dog, a boxer named Ben. No matter how hard they tried, they could not get the children to go to sleep on Christmas Eve.

I am sure that you all remember that when Santa come to visit you each Christmas, you all have to be in bed and fast asleep or he cannot leave any presents.

Well, for the last three years he had not been able to leave presents for the Turnbull children. They had all been awake. To make up for the disappointment of no presents, Mr and Mrs Turnbull had to go out on Boxing Day and buy them new presents. But what made the situation so much worse was that the children said that they did not believe in Santa any longer. Imagine not believing in Santa Claus any more   How sad. Something had to be done.

Santa decided that this was the chance for 'Bindlewith' to make up for all the problems he had caused with his mad over-enthusiasm.

Santa called him into his sitting room, sat him down in a comfortable chair and explained the situation with the Turnbull children. He asked him to take the small sleigh with two of the spare reindeer, pack a bag of sleeping dust and head off early on Christmas Eve to the Turnbull house. Santa told him how important it was for him to slip into the house unseen and unheard, creep quietly into the children's bedrooms and before they were aware, blow sleeping dust into their eyes so that for the first time in three years Santa could leave the presents they had asked for when they wrote their Christmas list.

'Bindlewith' was excited and proud at the responsibility he had been given and took his task very seriously. Early on Christmas Eve we waved our happy elf off on his important mission. The sleigh soared away and within seconds had vanished into the night sky.

It was dark and cold when the sleigh landed softly on the roof of the Turnbull house. The little elf slid quietly down the chimney, bag of sleeping dust in his hand. He crept across the sitting room and listened carefully at the foot of the stairs. All he could hear was the sound of Mr Turnbull quietly snoring up in the master bedroom. He could hear no noise from the children's room. Perhaps they had at last fallen asleep.

'Bindlewith' moved silently up the stairs and was listening outside Simon and Mark's bedroom door when he heard a growl behind him. Suddenly chaos broke loose and the elf was pinned under the paw of Ben, the very large boxer dog who was now barking his head off.

A few seconds later the whole family were on the top landing and there was a barking 'Ben' and a screaming 'Bindlewith' pinned under a large paw. Mr Turnbull called 'Ben' off and Mrs Turnbull picked up a very frightened. quivering little elf.

Mrs Turnbull said that perhaps they should all go down to the kitchen to have a cup of tea to calm them down. Down they went. Mum and Dad had tea, the children had orange juice and 'Bindlewith' had milk. He spilled most of the first cup as he was still shaking. Eventually when the family recovered from the shock of meeting a real elf in their house Mr Turnbull asked 'Bindlewith' what he was doing there.

'Oh please' cried the little elf. 'I am 'Bindlewith', a Christmas elf. Santa has heard that the children were no longer believing in him because they were not getting any presents on Christmas morning and asked me to blow some sleeping dust into their eyes to make them sleep and then he would be able to deliver the presents and they would start believing in him once again. I have failed'. Tears began to run down 'Bindlewith's' face.

'Let me think for a minute' said Mrs Turnbull. They all sat quietly while she thought. I'll Tell you what we will do. 'If all the family will agree, we'll go to bed now. 'Bindlewith' can blow the sleeping dust into our eyes and perhaps this year we will get presents from Santa. Oh! And perhaps he should blow some dust into Ben's eyes too'. And that is just what they did.

'Bindlewith' flew back home happy and Santa was at last able to deliver the presents to the Turnbull family.

The children wakened in the morning and there at the foot of their beds and round the tree downstairs were all the presents Santa had left.

Later at breakfast, Simon said: 'Do you know, last night I dreamed the strangest dream about an elf .' 'That's very weird,' said the rest, 'so did we.' Suddenly the all realised that it had been no dream. It really had happened.

After his exciting experience, 'Bindlewith' has settled down and is now one of Santa's best elves.

The family have all grown up and do you know, like you, they all still believe in Santa Claus.

2 HOW RUDOLF GOT HIS RED NOSE

This story begins like all good stories begin with, Once upon a time. The difference is that this is not a fairy tale. This story is true.

Once upon a time, many, many years ago, near the beginning of time, Father Christmas and the elves were getting ready for their Christmas Eve delivery of presents to children all over the world. The sleigh had been brought out and had been carefully inspected by the chief mechanic elf, 'Kafar Zyton' but everyone called him 'Spanner' as he was the best mechanic to be found anywhere in the Galaxy. The runners had been polished until you could have seen your face in them and the harnesses gleamed a shiny red and black.

The Reindeer were fit and ready to go, thanks to the efforts of 'Vanderith', the chief Reindeer herder. All the elves who look after the Reindeer are lady elves. They seem to understand the ways of the Reindeer better than anyone else.

All the Reindeer had been lined up and 'Vanderith' had whispered gentle words to each of them in turn. She spoke to Dasher, Dancer, Prancer, Donner and Blitzen, Comet, Cupid and Vixen. They were all very excited and ready for the long night ahead.

Father Christmas had been talking to 'Vanderith' earlier and they had been discussing the ever increasing load the Reindeer had to pull each year as the number of children expecting presents grew and grew. They decided to add one more Reindeer to the team. 'Vanderith' suggested a young Reindeer, new to the herd, called 'Rudolf'. Father Christmas thought he was a too young and a bit too small to be helping to pull such a heavy sleigh but 'Vanderith' insisted that he was really keen and ready for his big challenge. 'Vanderith' was the expert so Father Christmas gave in and agreed that 'Rudolf' should be the extra Reindeer helping to pull the sleigh that Christmas.

At last it was Christmas Eve. The sleigh stood gleaming in the snowy night, laden with presents. The Reindeer were tramping and snorting and pawing at the snow impatiently. The elves who had worked so hard all year making the presents for all the girls and boys were excitedly bouncing around waiting to wave the sleigh off. Father Christmas cannot deliver all the presents without help and he has a team who go with him each year. He needs to know where he is going and who he is delivering presents to and that is where his team of helpers come in. They don't use any sill old Sat Nav thing like mums and dads do. They use their eyses, earses and noseses.

Father Christmas has four elf friends in his team. They are: 'Eldar Pildoor' but they call him 'Goggle Eyes' as he can see forever and lets them know when they are near houses and if there are any sticky up things about that they might bump into.

'Achard Penduhl', known as 'Big Ears'. He listens for all the noises of the night and can hear if any of the children are awake. If they are awake they call back later. 'Secor Syr' or 'Sniffy'. He can smell danger for miles and he is really good at smelling out, mince pies, biscuits, chocolate, cookies and milk. He can even sniff out the carrots left out for the Reindeer. Then there is the beautiful 'Eloon Aldaren' or 'Stargazer'. She looks up into the night sky at all the brightly burning stars and she can tell exactly where they are and how long they have left to deliver the presents before dawn breaks and they have to go home for another year.

They all climbed into the sleigh and with a crack of the whip, they were off. Don't worry, the whip never hits the Reindeer. They just like the noise the whip makes when it is cracked.

Off they went up into the night sky, with the Reindeer bucking and prancing excitedly as they made their way to their first delivery.
They hadn't travelled far when it started to get a bit misty. It was nothing to worry about as there was often a bit of mist around on these cold and frosty winter nights. This was different. The further they flew, the thicker it grew until they could see nothing at all. They had to stop. They were in the middle of a thick blanketing fog and they were lost. 'Goggle Eyes' could only see the thick swirling fog. His eyes were useless. 'Big Ears' could hear nothing. It was like being surrounded by a thick ball of cotton wool. All 'Sniffy' could smell was the fog. His nose would not work and there were no stars for 'Stargazer' to see. What were they to do? Children would be waking up on Christmas Morning and there would be no presents under the tree or around their bed.

They sat in the sleigh in the middle of that huge night sky and they really were lost. They talked and they worried but they didn't know what to do. They could not go on and they could not go back and even Father Christmas had no ideas.

Suddenly 'Goggle Eyes' shouted 'What's that ahead of us.' 'Where?' they asked.   They could see nothing.   'There at the front of the Reindeer' cried 'Goggle Eyes.'

Slowly something began to glow red, softly at first and then it got brighter and brighter.   It was 'Rudolf's' nose.   As his nose glowed a brighter and brighter red, the fog began to part as if it was being burnt off by the power of a little Reindeer nose.   The fog slowly cleared and by the light of 'Rudolf's' nose they were able to deliver all the presents and there would be lots of happy children waking up on Christmas Morning.

The news of their adventure and 'Rudolf's' shiny nose reached home before them.   All the elves were really excited and they all wanted to know how the little Reindeer nose started to shine but no one could tell them.   It just seemed to be magic.

When they got home 'Rudolf's' nose went out.   It was back to normal. 'Vanderith' settled the tired Reindeer into their stables and gave them a good feed.   The others all sat down to their traditional Christmas Morning huge breakfast and then went to bed for a good long sleep.   It is very tiring delivering so many presents to children all over the world in just one night.

No one knows why 'Rudolf's' nose began to glow red on that foggy Christmas Eve but on every Christmas Eve since, just as the Reindeer are being harnessed up for the long night ahead, a little Reindeer nose starts to glow red and gets brighter and brighter.   It is 'Rudolf' ready to light the way for another year and help make sure that girls and boys all over the world waken up happy on Christmas Morning.

Now, the name of this story is 'How Rudolf Got His Red Nose.'   But the truth is, no one knows.   Perhaps it really was magic.

3 THE BUTTERCUP CHILDREN

When Santa first delivered presents, so long ago that no one can remember, the Queen of the Fairies gave him a book. It was big and covered in a shimmering gossamer cloth which seemed to change colour as you looked at it. The pages were edged with pure gold.

The first time Santa picked up the book he was amazed to find that it had no weight at all. It was like picking up a handful of pure, clear air. The covers felt warm to the touch and after a few seconds of holding it, softly glowing red letters began to show, spelling out, "The Name Book". This was the book which Santa would use each year when delivering presents to all the children of earth.

When a new child arrived it would magically be added to the book and its name would show in beautiful velvety black lettering. Strangely no matter how many names were added the book never got any bigger.

Santa and the Elves found it quite funny as they knew that even before the child arrived the mums and dads spent long hours discussing and sometimes even arguing over the name to give the new baby. Little did they know that the child had already been named in "The Name Book" and that is the name they would eventually give their little one.

Each year countless names were added to "The Name Book" and once a name arrived, it was there forever, it never left. Sometimes a name would begin to change. At first it would begin to fade and then slowly change to a soft glowing Buttercup yellow and a little Angel would appear by the name. These were the names of the children who were now asleep and would sleep on until the end of time.

On Christmas Eve just after the sleigh had been loaded and the Reindeer harnessed up, Santa and the Elves would gather round, bow their heads and close their eyes. Each one, in their own way, would remember the Buttercup Children who no longer needed presents.

Now, on a bright, sunny, summer day when children go into fields to pick Buttercups, they often play the game of holding the Buttercup under each other's chin to see the little yellow glow that appears there. What they do not know is that the little yellow glow is the memories of the Buttercup Children in Santa's name book who will never, ever, be forgotten.

4 SANTA'S LOST NAME BOOK

Once upon a time Santa was flying along on his way to visit some children in a little village deep in the countryside. He had just brought his small sleigh and two Reindeer, Dasher and Dancer. There was no need to bring the great big Christmas Eve sleigh with all the Reindeer as he was only carrying a few 'before Christmas' presents for some children who had been particularly good that year.

It was snowing quite heavily and Santa had "Eldar Pildoor" with him. He is the elf they call 'Goggle Eyes' because he can see forever and with all the snow about Santa thought that his eyes could be very useful.

Santa had his big book with him. You know, the one called the 'Name Book' with all the names of all the World's children in it. Santa had made a note of the children who would be getting a special visit later that day.

They were flying along quite happily with 'Goggle Eyes' at the reins. The snow was falling quite heavily and there were a few black clouds about. Suddenly a huge eagle swooped out of the snow. Dasher got a fright and pulled to one side. The sleigh bumped into one of the clouds and the 'Name Book' bounced out. Down and down it went quickly dropping out of sight. Well, this was a real problem. Luckily Santa had a note of the children he was visiting later that day but all the names were now lost of all the children who were to receive presents at Christmas. No book meant no names and no names meant no presents.

No harm had been done to the sleigh or the Reindeer so they carried on to their destination. Santa went to meet the children and sent 'Goggle Eyes' back with the sleigh to see if he could find the "Name Book" in all the thick snow. Much later 'Goggle Eyes' came back looking very glum. Even with his amazing eyesight he had not been able to find the book. The snow was too thick. There was nothing else for it, they had to go home without the book.

A few days later in a lonely farm in the hills, near the village Santa had been visiting, a little boy called George had built a beautiful big snowman. George had given the snowman twigs for arms, a carrot for a nose, little pieces of coal for eyes and had scraped a big smiley mouth on the snowman's face. To finish him off he stuck a slice of turnip on each side of his head for ears.

It was getting quite dark and George's mum called him in for bed. George took a hat and scarf from a hook behind the kitchen door and put them on the snowman to keep him warm and went inside. He was having a mug of hot chocolate before brushing his teeth and going to bed when he remembered that he had some Reindeer Dust left over from last Christmas and thought that he would sprinkle it over the snowman to make him sparkle.

He popped quickly out of the door and sprinkled what was left of the dust over the snowman who now twinkled and sparkled in the light spilling from the kitchen window. George said goodnight to the snowman, came back inside and thinking no more about it went happily to bed.

Much later George woke up. The house was still and quiet. George listened but the only sound he could hear was the ticking of the grandfather clock downstairs in the hall. Something strange had woken him but he didn't know what. Then George thought he heard a sound coming from outside. He crept out of bed, went over to the window and looked out. He couldn't believe his eyes and had to pinch himself to make sure that he was awake. Down in the yard, in the light from the full moon the snowman was waving a twiggy arm at him and calling softly, 'George, George.'

George put on his slippers and big warm dressing gown and went quietly downstairs trying not to disturb the rest of the house. He opened the kitchen door and slipped out into the yard. Snowman was standing there, twigs on hips and said to George: 'About time too. I thought you were never going to waken up.' George's mouth dropped open. 'Yyyyyou cccccan ssssssppppppeak and mmmmmove,' he stammered. 'Better than you can, it seems,' said the snowman. 'You can speak and move, so why shouldn't I. After all it was you who showered me in Reindeer dust and that gives snowmen life.'

George, by this time was getting over the shock of meeting a talking to a moving snowman for the first time and remembering his manners said, 'How do you do, my name is George.' 'I know that,' said the snowman shaking George's hand with his twig. 'How do you do too.' 'What is your name?' asked George. 'Most people call me Frosty but I much prefer my real name, which is Agamemnon Horatio Zapperdoodle White. The Zapperdoodle is from my mother's side and we all have the last name White, for some reason. You can call me Aga, it's shorter and seems warmer. But enough of this chitter chatter.' said Aga. 'Ho! Ho! Ho!' laughed Aga. 'That was a joke. Chitter chatter and it's cold.' George just managed to raise a weak smile as all this was beginning to make him feel very confused.

'We have work to do.' Said Aga. 'Oh!' Exclaimed George. 'Yes, if you look over there by the wall in the corner, you will see something sticking out of the snow. Bring it to me please.' Said Aga. George went over to the pile of snow and saw the corner of a very large book sticking out. He pulled it and it came unstuck very easily. Considering it's size it was amazingly light. George carried it over to the snowman. Aga took the book and scratching his chin with a twig said: 'Do you know what this is?' 'No' answered George. 'If I am not mistaken, this is a very important book.' said Aga. Aga handed the book back to George. It was very large but weighed almost nothing and was covered in a shimmering gossamer material which seemed to change colour as you looked at it. The pages were edged with pure shining gold. It did look a very important book. 'What does it say on the front?' asked Aga. 'My eyes aren't too good. You made them too small.' 'Sorry,' said George. 'It doesn't say anything.' 'Rub it a bit. It might be cold.' said Aga. George did as he was asked and as he rubbed, the cover of book started to get warmer. Red glowing letters began to appear. It said 'The Name Book.' 'I thought so,' said Aga. 'What is it?' asked George. 'It is the names of children all over the world that Santa will be delivering presents to on Christmas Eve. Without it there will be no presents. We must return it tonight and you can help by carrying the book,' said Aga. 'Why can't you carry it?' asked George. 'Feel it,' said Aga. George felt the covers of the book and they were quite warm. 'It is a magic book. Each year, new names are added by themselves and that is what makes it warm. If I carry it I will start to melt and by the time we get to Santa there would be nothing left of me and I am sure you wouldn't like that to happen,' said Aga.

Without another word Aga took George's hand in his twig and began to stride out through the farm gate and across the open fields. 'Can we not fly?' asked George. 'Don't be silly,' answered Aga. ' That was another snowman in a Fairy Tale and besides you didn't use enough Reindeer dust.' George had lived here all his life and knew all the fields, trees, hedges and hills as well as anyone could but tonight they all seemed just a bit different. The snow sparkled in the moonlight far more brightly than he had ever seen before and some of the shadows looked as if they were moving by themselves.

It felt as if they were trudging on forever and George was getting very tired and slowing down. Seeing this Aga bent down, picked George up, popped him on his shoulder and carried on through the snowy night. Eventually they came to a grove of trees that George was sure he had never seen before. In the middle of the trees stood a massive Oak with lights twinkling all over it and at the base of the giant trunk was a golden door. Aga opened the door and walked in as if he knew exactly where he was going. The inside of the tree was hollow and much bigger that it looked from the outside. All round the inside of the trunk were beautiful candles and little twinkling lights. It was like being inside a giant Christmas tree. In the middle of the floor was a big hole and a soft golden glow shone up from far beneath. Hanging down from up above was a cord, a bit like the one on George's dressing gown but much thicker and shining with all the colours of the rainbow.

Aga put George down and said, 'Hold onto the cord.' George was more than a little scared but clutching the book tightly did as he was told. Aga held the cord too and suddenly they were dropping. George felt as if he was floating, weightless as they dropped quickly down. It felt like forever but eventually the cord slowed and stopped. They were at the end of a huge hall. It was as long and wide and tall as the biggest cathedral he had ever seen on his school trips. The wooden pillars holding up the massive roof were as big as tree trunks and the great hall was lit by what seemed like thousands of candles in chandeliers hanging from the ceiling and all round the walls. There were lots of doors down either side, so many that George couldn't count them and right down the centre of the hall, almost running from one end to the other was a beautifully carved oak table. At the far end of the hall was a cavernous stone fireplace with a roaring fire blazing away. There were two huge golden chairs on either side facing the fire.

There were hundreds of Elves just sitting around in couches and chairs but George could hear no buzz of conversation, which he would have expected. Instead the elves were silent and looked so sad.

'What are you lot looking so miserable about?' Asked Aga. 'Oh Agamemnon' said one of the older elves, almost in tears. 'We have lost the Name Book and even GoggleEyes could not find it. What are we to do? Without it there will be no Christmas.

George, who was feeling very shy and overwhelmed by everything that was happening was trying to make himself as small and inconspicuous as possible, half hiding behind Aga and hoping no one would notice him.

Suddenly one of the younger elves spotted George and let out a delighted squeal. 'Agamemnon has found the book,' he squeaked, almost unable to talk he was so excited. 'Well, it was really George who found it.' Aga said modestly. 'If it hadn't been for him and his Reindeer Dust we would not be here'.

An excited buzz rippled down the great hall as the rest of the elves learned of the good news, the noise quickly getting louder and louder.

From one of the chairs by the fire a head popped out. It had flowing white hair and a great long silky white beard. 'Silence,' boomed Santa. 'This is serious. The Good Fairy and I are trying to discuss what to do and your noisy chatter is not helping.' 'But Santa,' cried one of the elves. 'But nothing,' boomed Santa. 'One more word and you will all go to bed. You all know what will happen if we don't find the book and that is unthinkable. So be quiet and let us concentrate.'

'Can I talk?' Another voice said. Santa stood up and came from behind his chair and so did the Good Fairy. George was having great difficulty taking all this in and was now completely hidden behind Aga.

'I haven't seen you for some time Agamemnon.' Said Santa. 'We have enough problems tonight, I hope you have not brought me more.' 'On the contrary. I think you need this.' Said Aga, pulling a very reluctant George from behind his back.

In spite of being told to be quiet, a great cheer rose from the excited elves all round the hall.

'Bring him to me Agamemnon,' said Santa. 'You are so far away that I can hardly see him.' 'I would rather not. It is already quite warm in here and that fire looks very hot.' Said Aga. 'Oh, we can soon fix that.' Said the Good Fairy and with a wave of her wand Aga was instantly surrounded by a cold blue haze. 'Thank you, Good Fairy, that feels so much better.' Said Aga. Aga took George's hand in his twig and to the sound of rousing elven cheers walked with him the length of the great hall to meet Santa and the Good Fairy.

When they got to the end of the hall Santa bent down and gently took the Name Book from George and laid it carefully on a side table. He took both George's hands in his and said: 'Young man, you have just saved Christmas and we are all more grateful than you will ever imagine. Without you and Agamemnon there would have been no presents ever again. Where did you find the book Agamemnon?'

'I was in the corner of George's yard.' Said Aga. 'I saw it fall but until George sprinkled me with Reindeer Dust I could not move. Once I could move I thought we had better get the book back to you as quickly as possible.'

The Good Fairy stepped towards the book and said: 'I think we had better make sure this can never happen again.' She waved her wand slowly back and forward over the Name Book speaking words softly in a tongue which George could not understand. 'Now George.' She said. 'Take the book and walk up the hall with it.' George picked up the book and started to walk up the long hall. At first the book was as light as before but the further he walked away from Santa the heavier the book became until it was so heavy he had to put it down on the table. As soon as he did this the book floated slowly up into the air and glided back down the hall to settle gently on the table beside Santa's chair. 'That should fix things,' said the Good Fairy smiling down at George.

'Now then,' laughed Santa. 'We cannot let this night go without celebrating the return of my Name Book. Elves, you know what to do.' And he clapped his hands.

No sooner had he done this than all the doors down each side of the hall burst open and elves came pouring out laden with trays of food. George had never seen anything like it. The table groaned with huge tureens of steaming soup, roasts of every kind of meat imaginable and puddings, jellies and cakes that defied description.

'George,' said Santa. 'As my guest of honour you must sit by me and Agamemnon can sit with the Good Fairy. He has always goes a bit soft when he sees the Good Fairy.' George could have sworn that if snowmen could blush, then Aga did just then.

Santa filled George's goblet with a wonderful fizzy drink that he had never tasted before but would never forget. Each time he had a drink his goblet magically filled itself up again. They all ate and drank and chatted until George thought he would burst and he was beginning to feel a bit sleepy.

Santa stood up and rapped his spoon on the table. 'I think it is time for a little speech,' said Santa. The elves groaned as they all knew how long Santa's little speeches could last but tonight it was mercifully brief.

'George my boy,' said Santa. 'Tonight with Agamemnon's help you have performed a service which is impossible to reward. The story of how you saved Christmas will be told in this great hall for the rest of time. I must give you something, however inadequate, to thank you and to help you remember what you did for all the children everywhere.

As I am sure you know, before I can deliver presents to any child, they must be in bed and fast asleep. You George are going to be the only exception. Every Christmas Eve from now on you can stay awake and if you look out of your window when you hear the bells on my sleigh, I will wave as I pass and in the morning, just like the rest of the children, you will find all your presents under the tree.' At this all the elves gave a huge cheer and threw their hats high into the air.

The grin on George's face was so wide that Aga thought that it might split. George was so tired now that he rested his head on his arms and in seconds was fast asleep.

'Agamemnon, the little lad has had a long tiring night. Perhaps you should take him home now,' said Santa

Aga picked George up, bowed to Santa and bowed even lower to the Good Fairy and still surrounded by the cold blue haze said goodnight to everyone and walking to the far end of the great hall held onto the silken rope and rose up to the world above.

The next morning George wakened with the sun streaming in through his bedroom window. 'Gosh!' He thought to himself. 'What a strange and wonderful dream I had last night.' He could remember every detail and it would not have taken much convincing to believe that it was real.

The sun was quite warm on his face and he wondered if the snow was still there. He got up and looked out of his window. The snow had all gone but in the yard stood the snowman. George was sure that the grin on his face was bigger than last night and he seemed to be surrounded by a strange blue haze.

George is a grown man now with a wife and two small children but still on Christmas eve when all the family are in bed asleep he stands by the bedroom window and remembers the night he took the Name Book back to Santa and saved Christmas. When he hears the sound of the sleigh bells he waves to Santa as he passes and as Santa promised, in the morning, all the presents are there under the tree.

5 SLEIGH TROUBLES

I am sure that many of you have heard of the poem 'The Night Before Christmas'. It begins:

'Twas the night before Christmas.

And all through the house,

Not a creature was stirring,

Not even a mouse.

Well, once upon a time, about a year ago in the big shed where Santa keeps the sleighs the mice had been stirring. Big mice with very sharp teeth. Kafar Zyton, the chief mechanic elf, the one we call spanner, came to see Santa to tell him that mice had chewed through the harnesses fitted to the big sleigh used to deliver all the presents on Christmas Eve. Now, these are no ordinary harnesses as they give the sleigh some of its magic powers and these powers help the reindeer fly with their heavy Christmas load.

The harnesses are woven from a magical metal thread called Transitomium. The ore to make this thread can only be found in Middle Earth in the mines at the base of Mount Tirich Mir in the realm of the Goblin King.

Nobody wants to go to the world of the goblins unless they really have to, as they have a fearsome reputation, but they had to get the ore, bring it back and refine it to produce the pure Transitomium which the elf blacksmiths would then roll thinner and thinner until it became as thin as the thread in a spider's web.

They didn't have any time to spare, so the small sleigh was made ready and Vanderith, the chief reindeer herder, harnessed up two of our strongest reindeer with an undamaged harness.

Santa asked Garanor and Dengord, his guardian elves, to go with him as goblins can be dangerous and unpredictable. Santa had to go too as he knew that the Goblin King, Biletooth would not talk to anyone else.

Off they went and using earth time it took them two long days to get there. Finally tired and hungry they arrived at the base of Mount Tirich Mir and

17

the entrance to the goblin mine which was guarded by two huge slimy Trolls.

The mine is not like any other. The entrance is a massive opening which leads to a huge cavern and in this mine is every precious metal and jewel you could ever imagine. Many greedy mortals have died trying to reach the mine and their bones are piled high outside the entrance. It is not a nice place to be.

They were met by the foreman, a large, rude, dirty goblin called Grubwort who said that Biletooth, the Goblin King, was expecting them and was looking forward to making them squirm and beg for the precious ore.

They were taken deep into the mountain going down and down past galleries of goblins chipping at the walls, extracting the jewels and metals to add to the vast stores of wealth they loved so much. Santa's two bodyguards were tense and looked for danger at every twist and turn. The goblins were not to be trusted.

They finally emerged into a massive cavern which was dimly lit by large spluttering candles. It was so vast, it was impossible to see from one end to the other. In the middle of the cavern, seated at an immense table and surrounded by other goblins was Biletooth.

'Welcome Santa' Biletooth sneered. 'I thought you were never going to get here. You must be hungry after your long journey. We were just about to dine so why don't you join us'. Now that is something you don't want to hear! We know that Goblins are quite ugly but they are also very dirty. They don't take showers. They don't brush their teeth. They are very smelly and they don't wash their hands after they've been! They eat things like Maggotburgers, boiled fish heads and spinach. But if Santa wanted the precious ore he could not afford to offend the Goblin King and so, had to sit down for dinner. It wasn't as bad as expected. It was even worse and to finish off they had to eat Frog Pond Slime for pudding. It looked a bit like green lumpy custard but the taste was horrendous.

'What is your price for enough of the ore to make a new set of harnesses for the sleigh' Santa asked Biletooth. 'Oh that is easy', he said, sitting back rubbing his huge tummy.'On Christmas Eve you never deliver all of the presents we have asked for , so my price is that this year you deliver all of the presents on our lists. If not there will be no precious ore, which means no sleigh, which means no Christmas'.

'But you always ask for far too much', Santa said. If I bring the Goblins all the presents on their lists, it will be almost impossible to find room on the sleigh for the ones I need to deliver to the rest of the children all over the world'. 'Too bad', said Biletooth. 'Take it or leave it. No presents, no ore, no ore no sleigh, no sleigh, no Christmas. It's up to you'.

Santa had no choice. Reluctantly he had to agree to the deal. 'Great', said Biletooth. 'Now off you go, back to your silly world'. 'But what about the ore? We have struck a bargain', Santa said, beginning to get a bit annoyed. 'Oh that', said Biletooth. When you get back you will find the ore already there. I knew you had a problem almost before you did. I have very good spies. I also knew that you had no choice but to agree to my demands, so I sent the ore off before you got here'.

'You mean I needn't have come', Santa said angrily. 'Oh no', said Biletooth. That was the fun part. You had to come and you had to squirm and beg and I did enjoy it. So off you go'.

Well, tired and with upset tummies Santa and the others left for the long trip home. When they got back, the ore had arrived. The blacksmith elves had already turned it into beautiful Transitomium and it was being rolled and stretched and changed into the gossamer thin thread which would be woven into the new harness for the big sleigh.

As for the problem with the number of presents they would have to deliver because of the greedy goblin demands, they solved that as well. There was enough Transitomium thread left over to make new harnesses for the small sleigh which they attached to the back of the big sleigh to hold all the extra presents and off Santa went round the world. Christmas had been saved once again.

6 THE CHRISTMAS ROBIN

This story is about one of my little feathered friends. The cheeky little red waistcoated Robin.

Like all good stories it begins with Once Upon A Time.

Once upon a time many years ago Santa was sitting in his big warm living room with Mrs Claus, the Good Fairy and some of the elves. There was a roaring fire blazing in the big fireplace and they were just sitting talking and sipping away at a nice after dinner glass of ginger beer. 'Santa' said Achard Penduhl, interrupting their conversation. 'Do you hear that?'. 'Hear what?', he said. Achard Penduhl is the elf we call Big Ears and if someone drops a pin 20 miles away, he can hear it. 'That knock at the door,' said Big Ears. 'Well if you can hear it you had better go and see who is there,' said Santa.

A minute later Big Ears came back and in his hand was the scruffiest, dirtiest little brown bird you have ever seen. His feathers were all ruffled and dusty and instead of a twinkle in his little black eyes there were tears.

'And who are you my little feathered friend? What makes you so sad?' Asked Santa. Oh Santa' the little bird chirped with a quivering beak. 'Do you not recognise me, I am Robin and you see me every day outside in your big garden looking for worms and grubs to feed me over the winter. A little while ago I was set upon by four very large Crows and they stole my beautiful red waistcoat. What am I to do?' 'We'll see about that' Santa said and sent Big Ears to the toy workshop to fetch all of the elves. When they returned he told them how serious things were and how they must help Robin get his red waistcoat back.

Santa asked them to get the sleigh out, harness up all the reindeer, including Rudolf and go out to search all of the woods hills and valleys around to find the bad crows and Robin's red waistcoat. The Good Fairy called all her fairies and as they had wings she told them to fly to all the corners of the earth to search for the lost waistcoat.

Mrs Claus felt very sorry for Robin and took him away to have hot drink and then she tucked him up in bed with Santa's best hot water bottle.

In the early hours of the next morning all the elves and fairies returned looking very tired and very sad. They had searched everywhere and had even been brave enough to ask the goblins in the dark forest and the trolls in the high mountains, but of the crows and the waistcoat there was no trace. What could be done? In a few hours Robin would be waking to a new day and would have to venture out a dull, drab brown little bird.

'Santa my dear' said Mrs Claus. 'If I get my wool out now I could knit Robin a new waistcoat and have it ready before breakfast'. 'Thank you' Santa said. 'That is a lovely thought but I am afraid that although your knitting is the finest and the lightest I have ever seen it will still be too heavy for little Robin'.

'I know' said big ears, clapping his hands excitedly. 'Shh' said Mrs Claus sternly. 'You will waken Robin with all that noise and then what will we do.' 'Sorry' said big ears. But we could weave cloth of the finest silk and then our tailors could make him the most beautiful waistcoat you have ever seen.' 'Another great idea' Santa said 'but it will still be too heavy for Robin to carry.'

'Well then' said the Good Fairy 'It would seem that it is up to me to solve the problem of the new waistcoat' She called her fairies together and told them to fly to the woods to search for the lightest and shiniest gossamer they could find. 'Bring enough back to spin the purest thread, dye it with the juice from the Christmas Holly and give it to the elf tailors.'

Off they went and in what seemed like the blink of an eye they were back with a huge ball of gossamer, so light that they had to hold onto it to stop it floating away. Soon it was spun, dyed, woven and made into the most beautiful red waistcoat in the whole world.

Mrs Claus wakened Robin, gave him a nice bath, oiled his feathers with special bird oils and took him down to breakfast. They were all sitting round the big dining table in the kitchen when Mrs Claus and Robin came in. 'I am very sorry' Santa said to Robin. 'The elves and fairies searched all night but sadly your waistcoat is lost forever.' Tears began to appear in Robin's eyes when the Good Fairy stood up. 'Cheer up my little Robin. We have a present for you.' With that she handed Robin a small golden box tied with a beautiful purple ribbon. Robin opened it and inside was a red waistcoat, so fantastic that words alone were not enough to describe it. Robin took it out of the box and slipped it on. It fitted perfectly. Magically it shimmered once and in seconds it was impossible to see where the feathers stopped and the red waistcoat began.

'Good Fairy, Santa, Mrs Claus and all my fairy and elf friends', said Robin. 'I can never find a way to thank you or repay you for your kindness this day but for as long as Robins live we will wear this red waistcoat with gratitude and pride.' And off he flew out of the open window.

The next time you see a Robin, especially in winter with his little red breast all puffed up. That is not because he is cold. His chest is swelling with pride at being able to wear such a special red waistcoat given to him by all his Christmas friends.

7 THE FAIRY HILL

It was the year 1823 and in a little village named Voe in the Shetland Islands two boys, Magnus and Lowrie were planning an escape.

The Highland Clearances had reached Shetland and many families were being evicted from their homes to make way for the big landowners and for sheep.

The boys were both 16 years old and like many young lads of their age, they were always up to some sort of mischief. The thing that the boys had in common, besides getting into bother at school and at home was music. They had learned to play the fiddle at the knees of their paternal grandfather and were now considered to be two of the best musicians in all the islands.

Magnus's family had secured employment with the new landowner but Lowrie's were not so lucky and were being evicted from their croft. The only two things left for them in Shetland were poverty and starvation and they had decided to sail to America to try to make a new life for themselves in the New World.

The boys hated the idea of being separated and true to their wild nature decided to run away. They intended to make their way to the main town of Lerwick and stow away on the first sailing ship that they could find.

Three days later the boys were hidden in the hold of the Dutch sailing ship 'Lelystad' bound for, they knew not where. All they had with them were their precious fiddles and a few potatoes to sustain them until they were discovered or managed to get ashore in one of the ship's ports of call.

Time passed slowly as there was no light to tell them the time of day or night and they were both suffering from seasickness as the little ship sailed through the stormy North Sea.

They must have been sleeping when they were awakened by the ship bumping against something and the sounds of many voices and lots of noisy activity.

Magnus and Lowrie managed to sneak on deck unseen to discover that the ship was alongside a quay at the mouth of a river but they had no idea where. They were hungry by this time and decided not to push their luck any longer and made their way carefully ashore unseen by the busy crew.

They went into a dockside tavern and bought some ale and bread with the little money they had with them and by listening to the conversation around them discovered that they were in the town of Inverness.

After much discussion they thought that the best thing to do would be to leave the town as they felt that there was a risk of being discovered there. They would try to find an inn in a quieter village ask if they could have a bed and food and in return they would entertain the guests with their fine fiddle playing.

It was a warm, late October afternoon the night before the feast of Samhain or Halloween as it is known now. The boys had headed west walking on the track beside the River Ness. They had walked for about two hours in fading light and realised that they would not find anywhere to stay that night. Ahead of them was a wooded hill and the boys thought that they could sleep there sheltered amongst the trees with little chance of being discovered and then move on the next day on the next leg of their journey.

They had just settled down quite comfortably with bracken for a pillow and wrapped up as best they could in their jackets when they heard a voice say, 'and what are you two rascals doing sleeping on my hill?'.

Startled, the boys jumped up to be confronted by a strange looking little old man. He had green breeches on and wore a bright blue tunic. On his head he had a red hat that looked just like a big bannock. His face had more than a passing resemblance to a wrinkled walnut.

'I am very sorry sir', stammered Magnus. 'We meant no harm and just wanted somewhere safe to sleep for the night'. 'Hmm!' said the little man, scratching his grey bristly chin. 'Are these fiddles that you have with you and are you any good with them?' 'We have been told that we are two of the best fiddlers in the whole of the Shetland Islands', replied Magnus. 'Would you like a warm and comfortable bed for the night then?' said the strange little man. 'Yes please', answered the boys.

'My name is Hreidmar and I am the keeper of this hill. Some local people call it 'The Hill of The Fairies' but that is just an old wife's tale. If you can play these fiddles as well as you say, you can have food and drink as well as a bed and perhaps even stay for a few days to keep my friends entertained'.

'Come with me', said Hreidmar and he walked towards a small yellow door set into the hillside that the boys had not noticed before.

They went through the door and walked down a long tunnel lit on either side by strange glowing lights that were neither candles nor oil lamps.

At the end of the tunnel was a huge oak door which slowly opened as they approached. They entered a beautifully decorated cavern hung with rich tapestries and lit by countless candles and lamps. There was a great feast going on and the guests were, like the old man, dressed in clothes the fiddlers had never seen before. Each suit and dress was finer than the one next to it. The fiddlers were duly fed and watered with some of the most sumptuous food and wine that had ever passed their lips.

Following this delightful meal the dancing started and the fiddlers began playing. Each felt that he was playing as never before and the notes coming from the fiddles seemed to emanate from somewhere not of this earth. Finally, in the wee small hours of the morning, the dancing and merrymaking came to an end and the fiddlers were thanked and off everyone went to bed.

This went on for many nights and the young fiddlers playing just got better and better. The boys were enjoying the company so much that they did not notice the passing of time but passing it was.

One night just as the boys began to play once again there was a noise like thunder from the end of the cavern and the massive oak doors burst open. There in the opening, in full war armour, stood Erlkonig the elf king and there behind him were the fairy queen and Father Christmas. The music stopped and there were gasps from all round the great hall as the three strode towards the head table.

Hreidmar sat there looking very startled, a wine glass half way towards his mouth. 'Hreidmar', roared Father Christmas, 'what have you done?' Father Christmas could get angry but it did not happen often. Tonight he was very angry with Hreidmar. 'We were just having a little fun' said Hreidmar weakly, looking very white and very scared. 'You know that time here and time in the world above are very different' said Father Christmas. 'What is going to happen to them when they go back to their own world?' 'We did not think of that' replied Hreidmar. 'Obviously not' said Father Christmas. 'Now, I will tell you what you will do. You will give them new fiddles as their old ones are worn out. You will furnish them with new clothes and you will give them enough wealth to make sure that they will never need for anything as long as they live.

In the world above it is Christmas Eve and I am going to be very busy but the good fairy is going to give Erlkonig human form and he will stay with the boys until they get used to being in a very different time. You, Hreidmar and your kin will forevermore stay sealed within this hill and will never again see the light of day'.

In the twinkling of an eye, Father Christmas and the good fairy had gone, leaving Erlkonig with a very bemused Magnus and Lowrie.   He tried as best he could to explain to the two boys that when they left the hill, things would have changed.

It was dark when the three of them emerged from underground and things were very different.   More than two hundred years had passed.   Where before there had been a dirt track with trees and fields, the track had become a wide black shiny road with big houses on each side.   Lights lined either side and strange carriages without horses moved along the road. Some of the houses had little trees in the windows covered with twinkling lights.

The boys were very confused and more than a little scared.   Erlkonig told them not to worry and just to stay quiet and to let him take care of things. He took a small flat thing from his pocket, spoke into it and shortly afterwards one of the carriages stopped beside them.   They got inside, where it was warm and very comfortable and Erlkonig told a man in the front, who was holding onto a big black wheel, to take them to the best hotel in town.

Once in the hotel they were taken to a huge room full of wonders they had never seen before.   If you pressed a thing on the wall the room was suddenly lit up.   In another small room you turned a lever and water flowed, both hot and cold.   There was a strange looking device in the corner with a lid on it and a handle on the side.   Magnus and Lowrie's eyes opened wide in disbelief when Erlkonig told them what it was for.   They had so much to learn.   Even the clothes they wore were strange but comfortable.

Erlkong sat the boys down and told them that they had been enchanted and that more than two hundred years had passed since they had entered the hill.   When they looked around them it was not difficult to realise that something strange and amazing had happened.   They were told to look in the bags that they had been given.   Inside were more strange clothes and a large leather pouch.   Inside the pouch was a large bundle of pieces of paper, some red, some blue with a picture of a lady wearing a crown on them and some numbers.   Earlkonig told them that it was called money and that they would find it very useful.   Also inside the pouch was a velvet bag containing three precious stones, a diamond, a ruby and a sapphire, each as big as a bird's egg.   'If you sell these at any time, you will have enough to live on for the rest of your lives.   Now, you must be hungry so I will get some food and then we can all have a good sleep.   The twenty first century can wait until tomorrow'.

The next day lessons began and for a week Erlkonig helped the boys explore the wonders of, for them, a new age. They learned about electricity, oil, transport, flight, the telephone, the internet, television and even space travel. It was a massive amount to absorb but the boys were still young and had minds like sponges.

'Well Magnus and Lowrie', said Erlkonig. 'My time here with you is almost over. You now know enough to start you new life in a new age. Take your time as there is still much to learn. I have one parting gift for each of you', and he gave each one of them a violin case. Inside was a violin which was dazzling to behold, inlaid in solid gold and studded with precious stones. 'In your time under the hill you have each become musicians the likes of which have never been heard before. Use this gift wisely'. With that Erlkonig slowly vanished leaving the boys apprehensive but very excited.

Time passed and they boys adapted well to their new life. Eventually they went their own way in the world but always kept in touch, seeing each other as often as time and commitments would allow.

Magnus discovered classical music and this became his life. He and his very special violin went on to entertain and enthral millions all over the world with his concerts and recordings. He never married. His music was all he ever wanted or seemed to need.

Lowrie eventually returned to Shetland, met and married a Shetland lass and spent many happy years passing on his talents to his own family and to young Shetland fiddlers, helping to keep this unique Shetland tradition alive.

If this was a real fairy tale, it would end with the two of them living happily ever after but that is not the way of the world.
The boys lived a long and happy life and as had been promised never wanted for anything. They both died peacefully in their sleep within days of each other and as they had asked, they were buried in the same grave on a hillside overlooking the shining waters of their home village of Voe, each with his precious fiddle alongside him.

It is said that on a warm summer evening if you are walking near Tomnahurich, The Hill of The Fairies, just outside Inverness, perhaps having a quiet stroll along the banks of the Caledonian Canal and you pause and listen you may hear fiddle music and the sounds of laughter and merriment coming from inside the hill.

Perhaps this really is a fairy tale and the boys did live happily ever after.

ABOUT THE AUTHOR

Robin Black has two of the best jobs in the world. In Summer while the Elves are busy making Christmas toys he is Captain of 'Sula II' in North Berwick, Scotland, taking tourists round the Bass Rock to see the largest rock colony of Atlantic Gannets in the world.
At Christmas he does his real job and with his big white beard and red suit delivers presents to children all over the world and sometimes telling stories. These are some of his stories.

Printed in Great Britain
by Amazon